The Fourth Floor Twins and the Silver Ghost Express

❦ BOOK REVIEWS

Here's what people are saying:

Hooray! A new young readers' mystery series by the same author as the popular **Cam Jansen** *series. The twins will be enjoyed for their clever sleuthing as well as their corny humor.*

from AMERICAN BOOKSELLER

A good dose of fun . . . . short chapters, lots of dialogue and action, and a good scattering of black-and-white drawings.

from THE BOOKLIST

Weekly Reader Books presents

The
Fourth Floor Twins

and the
Silver Ghost Express

DAVID A. ADLER
Illustrated by Irene Trivas

Viking Kestrel

Published by arrangement with
Viking Penguin Inc.

VIKING KESTREL

Viking Penguin Inc., 40 West 23rd Street, New York, New York 10010, U.S.A.
Penguin Books Ltd, Harmondsworth, Middlesex, England
Penguin Books Australia Ltd, Ringwood, Victoria, Australia
Penguin Books Canada Limited, 2801 John Street, Markham, Ontario, Canada L3R 1B4
Penguin Books (N.Z.) Ltd, 182–190 Wairau Road, Auckland 10, New Zealand

Set in Times Roman

Library of Congress Cataloging in Publication Data
Adler, David A.   The fourth floor twins and the silver ghost express.
Summary: Two sets of twins catch a thief while
tracking down a missing suitcase in a train station.
[1. Twins—Fiction. 2. Mystery and detective
stories] I. Trivas, Irene, ill. II. Title.
III. Series: Adler, David A.   Fourth floor twins series; #4.
PZ7.A2615Fod 1986   [Fic]   86-5552   ISBN 0-670-81236-6

To my niece Shira

CHAPTER ONE

"I have to water the plants," Max told Gary and Kevin Young. "And look, there are some smudges on the window. I have to clean them."

Max rushed across the lobby of the apartment building to his supply closet. Then he stopped.

"And don't forget," he told the boys, "if someone complains that his front-door key doesn't work, tell him to jiggle it."

Max is the doorman and fix-it man of the building. He was getting ready to leave for a short vacation. He was going by train to visit his brother George.

Max came out of the closet carrying a watering can and a rag. Max gave Kevin the watering can and said, "Please wipe the smudges off the windows."

"With this?" Kevin asked.

"Oh," Max said. "I must be nervous. I'm always nervous before I go on vacation." He took the watering can from Kevin and gave him the rag.

"You know," Gary said as Max was watering the plants, "when I'm older I'm going to be an inventor. I'll invent windows that don't smudge. And I'll grow camel plants. You know, camels can travel days without needing water. Well, my camel plants won't need water for a long time either."

"An inventor," Max said. "Last week you were going to be a bank teller. Before that it was a lawyer and a plumber."

"Bank tellers count money all day. After a while that gets boring," Gary said.

"The smudges are all gone," Kevin said as he handed the rag to Max.

The elevator door opened. Donna and Diane Shelton got off the elevator with their younger brother Howie and their mother. Howie ran across the lobby.

"Hi, Max," Howie said. "We're taking you to the train station."

"Are you ready?" Mrs. Shelton asked. "My sister's train is getting in at three-thirty. I don't want to be late."

"Yes, I'm ready. I just have to get my coat and suitcase."

Max walked into the supply closet. Then he stopped and looked up. "This light bulb has burned out. I have to change it."

"It can wait until you come back," Mrs. Shelton said. "If we get there late, my sister will worry."

Max put away the watering can and the rag. When he came out of the supply closet, he stopped. "Look," he said, and pointed to a corner of the lobby. "Look at what he's doing."

Howie was playing with one of the plants. He had torn off a leaf, and the floor was covered with dirt.

"I'll have to clean that," Max said.

Mrs. Shelton pulled Howie away from the plants. Then she told Max, "You get your suitcase. We'll clean this."

Max walked quickly across the lobby to his apartment. Mrs. Shelton took a broom and dustpan from the supply closet. She swept the dirt from the corner while Diane held the dustpan.

Tap. Tap.

Mr. and Mrs. Wilson were at the front door. Mr. Wilson was tapping on the glass.

"You have to jiggle it," Gary called through the door.

Kevin said, "They don't have to jiggle the key if we're standing right here." He opened the door for the Wilsons.

"Did Max leave yet?" Mrs. Wilson asked.

"Not yet," Max said as he came out of his apartment. He was wearing his coat and carrying a small suitcase.

"We want to wish you a good trip," Mrs. Wilson said. Then she whispered to Max, "And take an aisle seat on the train. That way, if you have to, you can get to the rest room in a hurry."

"What are you whispering?" Mr. Wilson asked. "Are you telling him to take an aisle seat? You tell that to everyone, and it's nonsense. Aisle seats are boring. There's nothing to look at. Max should take a seat by a window."

Mrs. Shelton opened the door and said, "We have to go now."

"Good-bye," Max said to the Wilsons.

Gary, Kevin, and Donna walked to the door.

"Wait," Diane said.

"What is it now?" Mrs. Shelton asked.

"It's Howie. He's gone."

CHAPTER TWO

"Howie! Howie!" Mrs. Shelton called.

No one answered. "Oh, I hope he didn't take the elevator somewhere," Mrs. Shelton said. "If he did, we'll have to look on every floor."

Gary and Kevin looked in the laundry room. Max and Donna looked in the mail room.

"Here he is," Diane said. She came out of the supply closet. Howie was right behind her, carrying a wet mop.

"I'm going to clean the floor," Howie said.

Mrs. Shelton took the mop from Howie and said, "You're not cleaning anything. We're going to the train station."

Mrs. Shelton held Howie's hand as she put the mop back in the supply closet. She still held his hand as they walked outside to the car.

The car was a station wagon. Gary and Kevin sat in the back. Max sat in the middle seat with his suitcase on his lap. Diane and Howie sat next to him. Donna sat in front with Mrs. Shelton. They all buckled their seat belts.

"What time is your train?" Mrs. Shelton asked Max as she started the car engine.

"Oh, not until five-thirty. I have plenty of time."

It was a long drive to the train station. After they had been in the car awhile, Max said, "While I'm away, I'll miss my fourth floor twins. And I'll miss you, too, Howie."

Max calls Donna, Diane, Gary, and Kevin his fourth floor twins because both sets of twins live on the fourth floor of the apartment building.

Donna and Diane are identical twins. But they try not to look exactly alike. Donna wears her hair in braids. Diane lets her hair hang straight down.

Gary and Kevin are not identical twins. Kevin has straight hair and freckles. And he's taller than his brother. Gary has curly hair and wears eyeglasses.

Kevin pointed out the window and said, "Look at the bumper stickers on that car. *Talk to your plants, but don't expect an answer.* And *Take a turtle to lunch.*"

"I like the one that says, *Marshmallows make great pillows*," Gary said. "If I had a marshmallow for a pillow and I got hungry at night, I wouldn't have to get out of bed."

Mrs. Shelton parked the car in a lot near the train station.

"Now listen to me, children," Mrs. Shelton said as she got out of the car. "I'm going ahead to look for Aunt Susan. Meet me in front of the big newspaper and magazine stand. I should be there in fifteen or twenty minutes."

"I'll show them where it is," Max said.

Mrs. Shelton walked ahead. Max held Howie's hand. Donna, Diane, Gary, and Kevin followed them into the train station.

It was a busy, crowded place. People carrying suitcases were rushing around. Others were sitting on long wooden benches and reading. There were many small shops along one side of the station where food, toys, books, and candy were sold. And there were announcements about trains arriving and leaving the station.

"Here's the newspaper stand," Max said.

He put down his suitcase near one of the benches. "You stay here with Howie," he told Donna and Diane. "I'm going to buy my train ticket."

Gary and Kevin walked off with Max. Howie began to follow them. Diane ran after him.

"Don't you run off," Diane said as she led Howie back to where Max had left his suitcase.

Donna and Diane sat on the bench. Howie watched a porter walk by pushing a cart loaded with suitcases. One small suitcase kept falling off the cart.

An announcement was made:

"Now leaving on Track Four, the Cannonball Express. All aboard!"

Donna said, "Let's play a quiz game. I brought some questions along." She reached into her pocket and took out some cards.

"What's the most popular flavor of ice cream?" Donna asked.

12

"Vanilla."

"That's right. Now, which farm animal is the smartest—the cow, the pig, or the horse?"

"Stop!" Diane called out. A cat was running through the station and Howie was following it.

Donna and Diane had begun to chase after Howie when a porter pushing a loaded cart passed in front of them. Right behind the porter was a young, thin man carrying a very large suitcase. Donna and Diane waited for them to pass.

"Now where's Howie?" Diane asked.

Donna and Diane ran around the newspaper stand. They looked into a few of the small shops. Then Donna stood on one of the benches and looked for Howie.

"There he is, at the orange juice stand."

Donna and Diane walked quickly to a large table in the corner of the train station. Howie was watching as the machine made juice. One at a time, the oranges rolled under a large knife that cut them in half. Then the orange halves were held by a metal claw and squeezed. Juice from the oranges dripped through small holes at the bottom of the machine and into a pitcher.

"Howie, what are you doing here?" Diane asked.

"Don't you run off again," Donna told him.

They each held one of Howie's hands as

they walked toward the newspaper stand.

"Did you see that? Did you see how that machine makes juice all by itself?" Howie asked.

"We saw it," Donna said.

Then Diane said to Donna, "I think it's the cow."

"What's the cow?"

"It's the answer to your quiz game. It's the smartest farm animal."

"No. The pig is."

As they walked toward the newspaper stand, Donna said, "This can't be where we were before."

"Why not?"

"I don't see Max's suitcase."

CHAPTER THREE

Diane said, "Maybe this isn't where we were sitting."

"No, this is the place," Donna told her sister. "We sat right next to the trash basket. I remember the smell."

"Well, maybe someone thought it was his suitcase and took it by mistake. Do you remember what it looks like?"

Donna thought for a minute. Then she said, "It's small. I remember wondering how

Max could get everything into such a small suitcase."

"And it's brown," Diane said. "When I was sitting next to Max in the car, I noticed that it was the same color as his coat."

Donna and Diane looked at the people sitting on the bench near them. No one had a brown suitcase.

"Look," Donna said, and pointed. "There's a woman with a brown suitcase."

Donna ran after the woman. Diane began to follow her. Then she realized that Howie wasn't with them. He was at the newspaper stand shaking a small box of candies. Diane ran up to him.

"Is this your boy?" the woman at the newspaper stand asked.

"He's my brother."

"Well, keep him away from here. He's messing up the candy display."

Diane took the candy box out of Howie's hand and put it on the rack. "I'm sorry,"

she told the woman as she led Howie away.

"Why do you keep walking off?" Diane asked him. "And why do you touch everything?"

"I wanted to buy that candy. I just didn't have any money."

Donna had stopped the woman carrying the brown suitcase. "Are you sure this suitcase is yours?" Donna asked.

The woman smiled and said, "Do you see this?" She pointed to a large stain on one side of the suitcase. "I made that stain a long time ago. The train I was on stopped suddenly and I spilled my coffee. I was about to clean it, but I saw the stain was in the shape of a rabbit. I named the rabbit Fluffy. He's traveled all over the world with me."

Donna, Diane, and Howie walked slowly through the train station. They saw a few brown suitcases. Most of them had name tags attached. A few were very big. None was Max's.

They saw a man carrying a small suitcase with two windows in it. A small dog was inside. Howie was about to put his finger

through one of the windows when Diane stopped him.

They also saw a worker carrying a large letter *B*. Behind him were five other workers carrying the letters *A, K, E, R,* and *Y.* A young, thin man passed them carrying a suitcase that seemed much too big and heavy for him. And a girl passed carrying a tuba.

When they were back at the bench near the newspaper stand, Diane asked, "What are we going to do? We've looked everywhere. What are we going to tell Max?"

Donna said, "We better think of something real fast. Here he comes."

CHAPTER FOUR

When Max saw Donna and Diane, he walked quickly toward them. Gary and Kevin had to run to keep up with him.

"I have my tickets," Max told the girls. "I bought a round trip. It was cheaper. My train is called the Silver Ghost Express. It leaves at 5:38. Oh, I can hardly wait to see George."

"Max, we have to tell you something," Diane said softly.

"My train arrives at 8:12. I called my brother and told him. He said he'd meet me at the station."

"Now leaving on Track Two, the Blue Fox. All aboard!"

Diane said, "Max, we *really* have to tell you something."

But Max kept talking. "I bought this magazine. Look who's on the cover—Princess Di. There's an article in here all about her children. And there's an article about the five richest people in the world. It's all about their hobbies and things. I'll read it on the train."

"Max," Diane said again softly, "what we have to tell you is important."

"The train goes through some beautiful country," Max said. "I'm going to enjoy the ride."

Donna stamped her foot and said in a really loud voice, "Listen, Max. Your suitcase is gone. We don't know where it is.

We looked, but we couldn't find it."

"Gone!" Max said, and sat on the bench. He shook his head. "I knew it. I just knew something would go wrong. I thought something would go wrong in the apartment building. I never thought I'd lose my suitcase."

Kevin said, "We can't just sit here. Let's look for it. Let's do something."

"I had everything in that bag," Max said. "I had my clothing, my electric shaver, and

a present for my brother. I bought him some mystery books. The books were wrapped in real nice gift paper."

"We'll find it," Kevin said. "We'll look everywhere."

Gary said, "Now tell us, Max. What does your suitcase look like?"

"It's brown. Not too big. And there's some green tape on the handle. The handle broke, so I taped it."

"Someone may have taken it by mistake," Gary said.

"I think someone stole it," Donna told the others. "And I'll bet that right now he's reading one of the mystery books Max bought for his brother George."

Max said, "There must be some police around here or a lost-and-found department. I'll report that my suitcase is missing."

"And we'll look for it," Kevin said. "I think we should split into two groups. Gary and I will look up here in the waiting area. Donna and Diane can look downstairs, where the trains are."

Diane said, "We'll take Howie with us."

Max, Gary, Kevin, and Donna began to walk off. Diane turned in a circle. She stood on the bench and looked. Then she called to the others and said, "I can't find Howie."

CHAPTER FIVE

"Howie is gone!" Max said. "We have to find him."

"We'll look for him while we look for your suitcase," Gary said.

"Oh, no," Max said. "We'll just look for Howie. Finding him is much more important than finding my suitcase."

Max thought for a moment. Then he said, "I'll report that he's missing. I'll have it announced over the loudspeaker. Was he wearing his blue jacket?"

"Yes," Diane answered, "and brown pants and a blue-and-red stocking hat with a little pom-pom on top."

Max told the twins, "You do just what Kevin said. Split into two groups and look for him. After the announcement I'll wait here. Maybe he'll come back."

A porter walked by. He was pushing a cart loaded with suitcases.

"Are there any police here, or a lost-and-found?" Max asked.

The porter stopped pushing his cart. "What did you lose?" he asked Max.

"A small boy."

"Oh, my," the porter said. "You go straight past all these shops. Then, just before you come to the flower stand, turn left. You'll see the office. Don't worry. They'll find your boy."

"Thank you," Max said. The twins

watched as he walked quickly past the shops.

Kevin and Gary were about to begin looking for Howie, when Diane said, "Let me tell you where to look. Howie likes animals. If he sees a dog or a cat or a bird, he follows it. He likes candy, cake, cookies, and ice cream. He likes to see how things work. He might stop to watch a machine make orange juice or he might watch a plumber fix a toilet."

"I know," Kevin said. "He might be any-where."

"Now leaving on Track One, the Purple Goose. All aboard!"

Gary and Kevin walked slowly through the waiting area. They looked behind suit-cases and under benches.

"Maybe he's in one of the stores," Gary said.

The boys looked in the toy store. Then they went into the candy store. Kevin walked to the back of the store and looked around.

Gary looked at the jelly bean jars.

"I have them sorted by colors," the man behind the counter said.

Gary looked at the gumdrops. They were sorted by colors, too.

"Most people like the red gumdrops best. But I like green and yellow," the man said.

Gary said, "I like them all."

"Let's go," Kevin said, and started to leave the store.

Gary took one last look at the jelly beans and gumdrops. Then he followed his brother.

Near the candy store was a wall of lockers. Gary and Kevin saw people open the locker doors and put their suitcases inside.

While Gary and Kevin were looking for Howie, they heard a man say, "That's my suitcase, but I didn't leave it here."

A small suitcase was under a bench across from the lockers. The man took the suitcase and walked with it toward the track area.

Just as Gary and Kevin were leaving the

lockers, a young, thin man carrying a large suitcase rushed past them.

Then Gary and Kevin stopped to listen to an announcement. Donna and Diane were downstairs, where people were rushing onto trains. They stopped and listened, too.

"Attention, travelers. Attention. Please look out for a little lost boy. He's wearing a blue jacket, brown pants, and a blue-and-red hat. If you see him, please tell the nearest guard."

"Someone will find him," Diane said.

Donna and Diane were standing near the open door of a train. A conductor was standing there, checking people's tickets.

"Excuse me," a man said to the conductor. "Have you found a small green suitcase?"

"No, I haven't. You should check at the office. It's on the upper level, right before the flower stand."

"We're looking for a lost boy," Donna told the conductor. "He's our brother."

"I'm sorry. I haven't seen any lost boys."

"Come on," Diane whispered. "Let's look upstairs. Maybe Gary and Kevin found him."

As Donna and Diane walked toward the stairs, a man rushed up to them. "Is this Track Four?" he asked.

"No. It's Track One," Donna told him.

The man turned around and ran back up the stairs.

A woman with long blond hair ran past

Donna and Diane. "Hold that train!" she yelled as she ran.

"Everyone is in such a hurry here," Diane said.

Donna and Diane walked up the stairs. When they got to the top, they saw Gary. He was running, too. "Come with me! Come quickly!" Gary called to the girls.

CHAPTER SIX

"What happened?" Donna asked.

"It's Howie. Your mother found him."

Diane ran after Gary. Donna walked more slowly.

Max, Kevin, and Howie were standing near the newspaper stand. Mrs. Shelton was there, too.

"Where were you?" Diane asked Howie.

"I was with Mommy."

"There's a large sign that lists when all

the trains arrive and leave. Aunt Susan's train was late, and I went there to see when it's coming in. That's where I found Howie."

"I like watching the numbers change," Howie said.

"We were watching him, but he kept running away," Diane told her mother.

Mrs. Shelton said, "As soon as I found Howie, I brought him here. I knew you'd be worried. But when I got here, you were gone."

"We were looking for Howie," Gary said.

"Now we have to look for Max's suitcase. It's missing," Kevin told Mrs. Shelton.

"Oh, my," Mrs. Shelton said.

Mrs. Shelton looked at her watch and said, "Oh, I have to go to Track Four. Aunt Susan's train is due in five minutes. I want to be there when she arrives."

Mrs. Shelton walked away quickly. Then she stopped and came back. She took Howie's hand and said, "I'm taking you with me.

Max and the twins will be busy enough looking for that suitcase. They don't want to look after you, too."

"Max, what are you going to do now?" Diane asked.

"I'm going to the office to report the missing suitcase."

Max and the twins began to walk across the waiting area.

"I'm going to invent a suitcase with a radar handle," Gary said as they walked. "You'll be able to find it anywhere."

A young, thin man passed. He was struggling with a very large suitcase. It seemed much too heavy for him.

"And it won't matter how much stuff you put in my suitcase. You won't have to carry it. It will have wheels and a motor. It will follow you to your train."

As Max and the twins walked past the candy shop, they heard someone call out, "Hey, where's my suitcase!"

Max and the twins turned and watched as an older man called to one of the porters. The man was wearing a dark gray suit and necktie. His coat, hat, and shoes were dark gray, too.

"My suitcase is missing," the man dressed in gray told the porter.

"I didn't take it," the porter told the man.

"It's a small gray leather suitcase with brass buckles. All my business papers are inside that bag."

Max walked up to the man and said, "My suitcase is missing, too. I'm reporting it to the office. Why don't you come with me?"

"Just walk to that flower stand and turn left," the porter said.

The man dressed in gray walked with Max and the twins. "Why would anyone steal my business papers?" the man asked. "They're just page after page of numbers. The thief won't understand them. Most of the time even I don't understand all those numbers."

"Whoever stole your suitcase won't know what's inside until he opens it," Donna said.

The man dressed in gray stopped walking and looked at Donna and said, "You're right."

Max walked into the office. The twins and the man in gray followed him. A woman dressed in a blue-and-black uniform was sitting behind a large desk. "Did you find your little boy?" the woman asked Max.

"Yes, we found him," Max said. "But my suitcase is missing."

"Yours is the seventh missing suitcase reported in the last hour."

"Mine is the eighth," the man in gray said.

"A few suitcases are reported missing every day," the woman said. "So many of them look alike. But I've never had eight in one hour."

The woman took a sheet of paper from a folder. Max told her his name and ad-

dress. Then Max described the missing suit-case.

"It's brown. It's small. And there's some green tape on the handle."

"That's interesting," the woman said. "All seven of the missing suitcases are small."

"All eight," the man in gray said.

There was a small bench against the back wall of the office. Kevin sat on it. He looked up at the ceiling and thought. Then he said, "I think I have it."

"What do you have? Do you have my suitcase?" the man in gray asked.

"No. But I think I know who does."

CHAPTER SEVEN

"This whole mystery is like a jigsaw puzzle," Kevin said. "And I think we have all the pieces. We just have to put them together."

"What is he saying?" the man in gray asked Max.

Max shook his head. He didn't know.

"All the suitcases that were taken are small. That's one piece of the puzzle," Donna said.

Then Kevin said, "And while we were looking for Howie, I heard a man say, 'That's my suitcase, but I didn't leave it here.' He found it under a bench across from the lockers."

"And it was a small suitcase," Gary said.

"Well, then, let's go," the man in gray said. "Let's look there."

The man left the office. Max, Donna, Diane, and Gary followed him.

"Wait," Kevin called. "There are some more puzzle pieces."

But they didn't wait. Kevin got off the bench and ran after them.

The man in gray and Max were walking quickly. The twins had to run to keep up with them. When they reached the locker area, they all looked under the benches.

"Is this yours?" the man asked and held up a small green suitcase.

"No," Max said and shook his head.

"Here's another one," Diane said. She

43

was holding a small blue-and-white bag.

"There are two here," Gary said. He held up a small red suitcase and a gray leather one with brass buckles.

"That's mine," the man in gray said.

Gary gave him the bag. The man sat on a bench and opened it.

"Look at this," he said, and held up some wrinkled papers. "Someone was looking in here. He made a real mess."

He put the papers back and closed the

suitcase. He thanked Max and the twins for their help. Then he looked at his watch and said, "I have a train to catch," and rushed off.

"Keep looking," Max said. "Mine should be here somewhere."

Max and the twins looked under all the benches. They found another suitcase. But it wasn't Max's.

Max sat on one of the benches. He shook his head and said, "My train leaves in twenty minutes. We won't find my suitcase. I'll have to borrow clothing from George, and he's two sizes bigger than me. I'll look terrible."

There was a rest room on each side of the lockers. Diane pointed to them and said, "Maybe the thief hid the other bags in there."

Max waited on the bench while the twins looked in the rest rooms. Donna and Diane came out first. "There weren't any in the women's room."

Then Gary and Kevin came out. They

were each carrying a small suitcase. Gary's was brown and had green tape on the handle.

"That's mine," Max said.

Gary brought the suitcase to him.

"Now I don't have to wear George's baggy pants. And I have my electric shaver and all those mystery books to give George."

"I don't think so," Kevin said. "I don't think everything is still in there."

"What? What's missing? How do you

know something is missing?" Max asked.

"Why would anyone steal all these suit-cases and then leave them here? He prob-ably went through them and took out what he wanted."

Max sat down on the nearest bench. He opened his suitcase, looked in, and said, "The clothing is all here. But the present is gone. And my shaver is gone, too."

Kevin said, "And I think I know who took them."

CHAPTER EIGHT

"It's a man," Donna said. "I know that because you found suitcases in the men's room, but there weren't any in the women's room."

"When we were looking for Howie," Kevin told Max, "someone left here carrying a real big suitcase."

"So?"

"It was too big to fit into any of these lockers."

"I remember him," Gary said. "When he left here, he was running with the suitcase, like it was real light. But later on he was carrying the same suitcase, but it was heavy. I remember because that's when I said I'd invent a suitcase that you wouldn't have to carry. It would have wheels and a motor."

"That's right," Kevin said. "How could the same suitcase be light sometimes and then heavy? I think he takes small suitcases and puts them into his. He brings them to the locker area because not too many people pass through here. He takes what he wants from the stolen suitcases. He leaves them here and then steals another one."

"What does he look like?" Max asked.

"He's young and he's real thin," Gary said.

"He's wearing a blue jacket and black pants," Diane said. "We saw him, too. When Howie ran off the first time, that man walked right in front of us. I remember that big suitcase."

"Let's go find him," Max said.

Max and the twins left the locker area. They looked for the young man in the blue jacket. Donna and Kevin stood on a bench.

"I see Aunt Susan," Donna said. "Mom and Howie are with her."

"And I see the man with the real big suitcase," Kevin said.

Kevin jumped down from the bench. He rushed toward the center of the waiting area. Max and the others followed him. As they hurried toward the young man in the blue jacket, they saw him stop next to a small suitcase. He very quickly pushed the small bag into an opening on the side of the big suitcase.

"I'll watch him," Max told the twins. "You get a guard."

The twins found a guard. He already knew about the missing suitcases. At first they couldn't find Max and the young man with the big suitcase. Then Diane remembered about the locker area.

"He's probably there now, looking through the suitcase he stole."

They all quickly went to the lockers. Max was hidden in a corner. The young man had taken an electric hair dryer and a jewelry box from the suitcase he had stolen. He was reaching into his pocket when the guard walked up to him.

"We have you now," the guard said. Then he called on his walkie-talkie for other guards to help him.

"Where's my shaver and my present for George?" Max asked the young man.

"I don't have any shaver. I don't know what you're talking about."

"Take that hand out of your pocket," the guard told the young man.

There was a key in the young man's hand. Three other guards came running

into the locker area. One took the key.

"This is a locker key," he said. "Number 557."

The guard opened Locker 557.

"Hey, look at all the stuff in here."

"There's my shaver, and my present for George," Max said.

The guard gave Max his shaver and the present. Then he told the others, "Let's take him to the office. Take all these suitcases and the stuff in that locker, too."

As they led the thin young man in the blue jacket away, one of the guards thanked Max and the twins.

After they were gone, Max looked at his watch. "Hey," he said, "I have to hurry if I'm going to make my train."

Max ran through the waiting area. The twins were right behind him. He ran down the stairs to Track Three.

"Hold that train!" Max called as he ran. "Hold the Silver Ghost Express!"

The twins watched from the top of the stairs. Just as the doors were closing, Max got on the train.

"Let's go find Mom and Aunt Susan," Diane said.

The twins walked toward the newspaper stand. Aunt Susan rushed to meet them.

"You've both gotten so big. Now, just wait until we get home. I've brought presents for all of you. That's right," Aunt Susan told Gary and Kevin, "I've brought something for you, too."

Aunt Susan and the twins walked to the newspaper stand. Mrs. Shelton was waiting there with Howie.

"Let's get a treat," Aunt Susan said. "How about some ice cream?" she asked the twins.

"I'll take vanilla," Donna said. "It's the most popular flavor."

As they started to walk toward the ice cream shop, Diane stopped and asked, "Where's Howie?"

"There he is, watching the orange juice machine," Kevin said. He went to get him.

"And where's your suitcase?" Diane asked Aunt Susan.

Aunt Susan looked down and said, "Oh, I hope I didn't leave it on the train."

"No, you brought it with you," Mrs. Shelton said. "I saw you put it next to the bench."

Aunt Susan went back to get her suitcase.

"Mom," Diane said, "I think we should go home."

Donna said, "We can get ice cream some other time. Let's go before we *really* lose someone or something."

Kevin came back with Howie. Then Aunt Susan joined the others. She had her suitcase.

"Well," Aunt Susan said, "let's get that ice cream."

"I want mine with lots of flavors and sauce and nuts and whipped cream," Howie said.

"We're not getting ice cream. We're going

home," Mrs. Shelton told Howie and Aunt Susan.

"What?" Howie asked.

"We're going home," the twins all said together.

"We have ice cream at home," Mrs. Shelton told Howie. "And I'm not afraid you'll get lost there."

Mrs. Shelton held onto Howie's hand. Aunt Susan held onto her suitcase. And the twins followed them out of the train station.

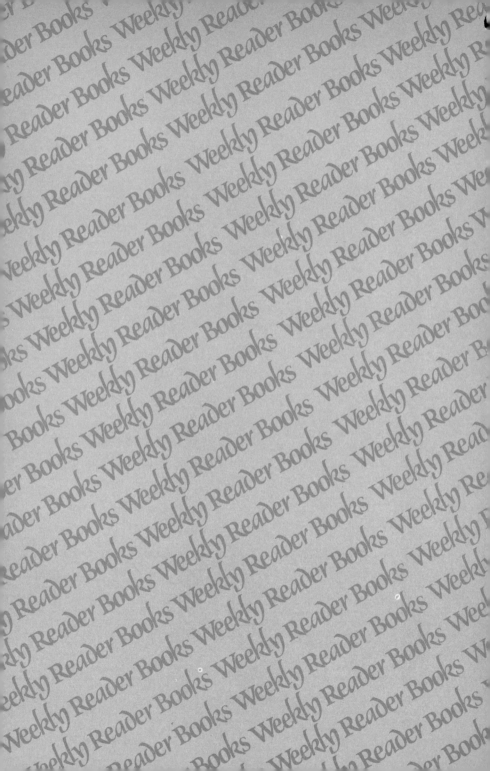